Clarinet part

the best of grade 2
Clarinet

A compilation of the best Grade 2 clarinet pieces ever selected by the major examination boards

Selected and edited by Paul Harris

© 2010 by Faber Music Ltd
This edition first published in 2010
Bloomsbury House 74–77 Great Russell Street London WC1B 3DA
Music processed by Jackie Leigh
Design by Økvik Design
Printed in England by Caligraving Ltd
All rights reserved

ISBN10: 0-571-53422-8
EAN13: 978-0-571-53422-7

To buy Faber Music publications or to find out about the full range of titles available
please contact your local music retailer or Faber Music sales enquiries:

Faber Music Limited, Burnt Mill, Elizabeth Way, Harlow CM20 2HX
Tel: +44 (0)1279 82 89 82   Fax: +44 (0)1279 82 89 83
sales@fabermusic.com   fabermusic.com

The text paper used in this publication is a virgin fibre product that is manufactured in the UK
to ISO 14001 standards. The wood fibre used is only sourced from managed forests using
sustainable forestry principles. This paper is 100% recyclable.

All audio tracks recorded in Buckingham, January 2010
Performed by Jean Cockburn (Clarinet) and Robin Bigwood (Piano)

Engineered by Robin Bigwood; Produced by Fiona Bolton
℗ 2010 Faber Music Ltd © 2010 Faber Music Ltd

Contents

The performers

Jean Cockburn studied the clarinet with John Davies at the Royal Academy of Music. She has established and performed in many successful chamber ensembles and is an experienced soloist and teacher. Recently she has edited the clarinet works of Alan Richardson for publication.

Robin Bigwood is a freelance pianist and harpsichordist, performing with Passacaglia, Feinstein Ensemble, Britten Sinfonia and as a soloist. He also works as a sound engineer and producer.

Track 1: Tuning note B (Concert A)

Ländler

from 'The Really Easy Clarinet Book'

Like a waltz, a ländler needs a strong dance-like character with a firm first beat to each bar and strong four-bar phrases. Sustain your tone through each note and create a marked contrast between *mf* and *f*.

PERFORMANCE 2
ACCOMPANIMENT 3

Anton Diabelli (1781–1858)
arr. Paul Harris

© 1988 by Faber Music Ltd

Greensleeves

from 'Clarinet Basics'

Avoid accents, starting each note gently to create a delicate and dreamy melody that floats along. Ensure each *crescendo* and *diminuendo* sounds natural and not forced.

PERFORMANCE 4
ACCOMPANIMENT 5

Attributed Henry VIII (1491–1547)
arr. Paul Harris

© 1998 by Faber Music Ltd

This music is copyright. Photocopying is illegal.

Lullaby

from 'First Book of Clarinet Solos'

This piece calls for repeated crossing of the break. Practise moving between B♭ and C until you can do so evenly and smoothly prior to working on this piece. Add more dynamic markings of your own for heightened expression.

Wolfgang Amadeus Mozart (1756–1791)
arr. Alan Richardson

Ländler

from 'First Book of Clarinet Solos'

Play this hearty and high-spirited dance with lots of vitality. You are accompanying the melody in bars 11 and 12, so play softly, listening to the piano. In performances with a pianist make the pause (bar 18) as long as you dare!

Carl Reinecke (1824–1910)
arr. Paul Reade

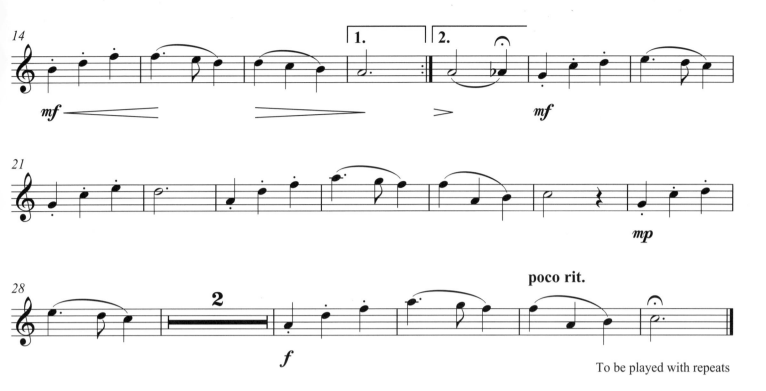

To be played with repeats

LIST A (ABRSM 2007)

The Merry Peasant

from 'First Book of Clarinet Solos'

PERFORMANCE [10]
ACCOMPANIMENT [11]

A jaunty and extremely cheerful tune. Practise the wider intervals carefully, aiming for well-coordinated finger movement. The short *p* passage can sound quite cheeky!

Robert Schumann (1810–1856)
arr. Paul Reade

To be played with repeats

The Babbitt and the Bromide

from 'Clarinet Basics Repertoire'

PERFORMANCE 12
ACCOMPANIMENT 13

A witty and charming number by one of the greatest American song-writers. The pairs of semiquavers must be tongued neatly and the chromatic passages (at bar 19 etc.) will require careful practice.

George Gershwin (1898–1937)
arr. Paul Harris

Allegretto humoroso

The Penguins Take a Stroll

from 'First Repertoire for Clarinet'

Try to paint a picture of the scene as you play this piece, using the many musical ingredients to bring it to life. The mood should be light-hearted and happy. Practise the low notes until they speak easily and with a full tone.

Paul Harris

Navaho Sunset

from 'The Really Easy Clarinet Book'

PERFORMANCE 16
ACCOMPANIMENT 17

A very evocative piece; another picture in music. Sustain the sound through the tied notes and make sure that the tone is full and round in the soft passages as well as the loud.

Paul Harris

LIST B (Trinity Guildhall 2007–11)

Solitary

from 'The Microjazz Clarinet Collection 1'

PERFORMANCE 18
ACCOMPANIMENT 19

A plaintive and rather sad melody. Maintain an even tone and avoid any accentuation.
Be careful to play the two semiquavers (in bar 5 etc.) in time and without rushing!

Christopher Norton

LIST B (ABRSM 1996)

Serenade: Beautiful Dreamer

from 'First Book of Clarinet Solos'

PERFORMANCE [20]
ACCOMPANIMENT [21]

Take care over the quality and length of notes just before taking a breath; try to breathe without anyone noticing! Aim to make the music really flow.

Stephen Foster (1826–1864)

To be played with repeat

Study No.16

PERFORMANCE 22

from '80 Graded Studies for Clarinet Book One'

Practise a two-octave scale of F major in preparation for this cheerful study. Play each note
staccato and try to give the music a bouncing quality; feel it as one-in-a-bar.

Friedrich Demnitz (1845–1890)

LIST C (ABRSM 2007)

Big-Brother Blues

PERFORMANCE 23

from 'Clarinet All Sorts'

A gentle jazzy number. Follow the dynamic markings carefully; notes marked with an accent
needn't be too heavy. Practise the second half of bars 9 and 11 slowly; don't move your fingers
more than is necessary.

Pam Wedgwood

Study No.15

from '80 Graded Studies for Clarinet Book One'

Practise the bars that cross the break, making sure that the tone is always sustained. Aim for a gentle flowing style with effective dynamic variation.

Henry Lazarus (1815–1895)

© 1986 by Faber Music Ltd

LIST C (Trinity Guildhall 1999–2002)

Dance

from 'Woodwind World Clarinet Book 2'

Give vitality to this jaunty tune and create contrast between the dynamic levels. Listen for a pure and well-focussed sound especially in the higher notes.

Jean Xavier Lefevre (1763–1829)

© 1994 by Trinity College London

Study in C

from 'Elementary School for Clarinet'

How many different arpeggios can you find in this study? Practise them all, aiming for well-controlled
and economical finger movement, then let the music spring along enthusiastically!

PERFORMANCE 26

Friedrich Demnitz (1845–1890)